W9-CCD-060

Please Don't Tell Cooper He's a Dog

Michelle Lander Feinberg

Illustrations by

Anna Mosca

Please Don't Tell Cooper He's a Dog, Published November, 2020

Cover Design: Howard Johnson
Interior Design & Layout: Howard Johnson
Illustrations: Anna Mosca
Editorial & Proofreading: Highline Editorial, New York, NY, Karen Grennan

Photo credits: Author photo owned by Michelle Lander Feinberg

Published by SDP Publishing, an imprint of SDP Publishing Solutions, LLC.
For more information about this book, contact Lisa Akoury-Ross at SDP Publishing by email at info@SDPPublishing.com.

SDP Publishing
Permissions Department
PO Box 26
East Bridgewater, MA 02333
or email your request to info@SDPPublishing.com

ISBN-13 (paperback): 978-1-7343317-2-1
ISBN-13 (hardcover) 978-1-7356973-7-6
ISBN-13 (ebook): 978-1-7343317-3-8

Printed in the United States of America

For Chili, Charlie, and Cooper, who rescued us as much as we rescued them.

In loving memory of Stephen Lander, whose home was filled with love and rescue dogs.

Come meet our dog, he's really quite super.

A thing you should know, though, about
our dear Cooper.

Please don't whistle or ask him to do a few tricks
as he thinks it's beneath him to chase balls or sticks.

He isn't embarrassed; he isn't ashamed.

The words "puppy" or "dog" just shouldn't
be named.

He's kind, and he's gentle, loyal, and brave,
but simply confused about how dogs behave.

Blame us if you will—he didn't start this way.

We found him at the shelter, picked up as a stray.

9

The jumping and nipping—
this hound was unruly!

And we saw in his eyes that
he was our dog so truly.

With training and love,
he soon fit right in.

Belly rubs and kisses
sure do make him grin.

His five human siblings shower
him with attention.

How he became so well-mannered,
I probably should mention.

Always treated like family, his parents' sixth child,
it became so unusual for him to be wild.

Dinnertime was for all; he joined when we ate.

No dog bowls for Cooper, he dined from a plate.

Spoiled for months—it's now been a year.

Cooper thinks he is human— this is so very clear.

15

At the dog park, he watches those silly pups play.

He'd rather be skiing or at the ballet.

As he chooses to lounge on our couches and chairs,
the dog bed we bought him has none of his hairs.

He couldn't be bothered with dog food or kibble
until we add steak sauce he won't even nibble.

Sure, for rides in the
car, he sits in the rear;
but that's only because
he kept trying to steer.

19

Seriously I say that he
thinks he's a person,
so please don't tell him
he isn't or his behavior
might worsen.

20

We tried to convince him
a couple of months back,
so he pooped in the toilet
then started to pack.

21

Hitched a ride to the airport and flew off to Spain.

After touring museums, he boarded the train.

Ate croissants in Paris, shopped in Milan.

Cooper started to realize how long he'd been gone.

Missing his family, it was time to return.

Made his way to Switzerland and took a plane
out of Bern.

We couldn't believe how far he did roam.

But as head of the family, of course, he came home.

23

Our lives without him would not be the same.
Our dog is a dog, but please, Cooper is his name.

The End

About the Author

Michelle Lander Feinberg is an attorney who lives in Massachusetts with her husband, Andrew, their five children, a dog, and a mouse. As a life-long animal advocate, she is a strong supporter of animal welfare organizations and does her best to spread the word of the importance of adopting pets from animal shelters and rescue groups.

About the Illustrator

Anna Mosca is an Italian illustrator. Currently, she is studying philosophy at the University of Genoa, plus art and illustration at the International School of Comics. She loves to give voice to characters, and make their fantasies come to life. Anna is an enthusiastic, humorous person full of creativity and determination. Her motto: "Head in the clouds but feet on the ground!"

Acknowledgments

I am sending my greatest appreciation to my editor, Robert Astle, of Highline Editorial, and my publisher, Lisa Akoury-Ross, of SDP Publishing Solutions, for all of your advice and for shepherding me through this entire process. Howard Johnson and Anna Mosca, your creativity and amazing artwork helped bring Cooper to life, thank you. I am grateful to my loving husband, Andrew, and to our five fantastic children, for your love, support, and honest feedback.

Information on Pet Adoption

Pets can be a wonderful addition to the family. Today there are many homeless animals that are looking for families to love! If your family is ready for a new pet, you can help find the perfect match at a shelter or rescue group. A great place to start online is a website that connects almost all of the shelters in one place, such as www.petfinders.com.

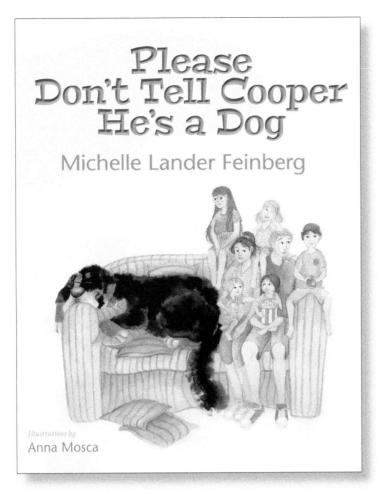

Please Don't Tell Cooper He's a Dog

Michelle Lander Feinberg

www.cooperthedog.com

Publisher: SDP Publishing

Also available in ebook format

Available at all major bookstores

www.SDPPublishing.com

Contact us at: info@SDPPublishing.com

9 781735 697376